Welcome to The Giggle Club

The Giggle Club is a collection of picture books made to put a giggle into early reading. There are funny stories about a contrary mouse, a dancing fox, a turtle with a trumpet, a pig with a ball, a hungry monster, a laughing lobster, an elephant who sneezes away the jungle and lots more! Each of these characters is a member of **The Giggle Club**, but anyone can join: just pick up a **Giggle Club** book, read it and get giggling!

Turn to the checklist on the inside back cover and tick off the Giggle Club books you have read.

TEE HEE!

HA HA!

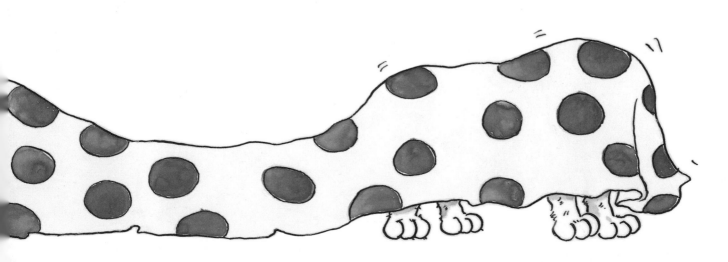

With thanks to Kate Weller! **J.H.**

For Rosina **P.C.**

First published 1998 by Walker Books Ltd
87 Vauxhall Walk, London SE11 5HJ

10 9 8 7 6 5 4 3

Text © 1998 Judy Hindley
Illustrations © 1998 Pat Casey

This book has been typeset in AT Arta

Printed in Hong Kong

British Library Cataloguing in Publication Data
A catalogue record for this book is
available from the British Library.

ISBN 0-7445-6085-3

THE BEST THING ABOUT A PUPPY

Judy Hindley

illustrated by Patricia Casey

WALKER BOOKS

AND SUBSIDIARIES

LONDON • BOSTON • SYDNEY

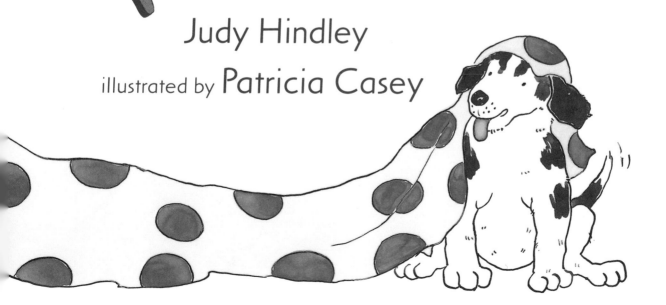

The good
thing about a
puppy is,
he's warm
and
wriggly.

The bad thing is,
he won't
keep still.

The good thing is,
the way he
rolls and
bounces.

The bad thing is,
he goes and jumps
in puddles – and that's
just when he bounces back,
and shakes himself and
wants a cuddle.

The good thing is,

you get to walk him every day.

The bad thing is,

he wants to go his own way.

The good thing is,
he loves to
chase a ball.

The bad thing is, he hates to
give it back.

The good thing is,
he likes to race
with you.

The bad thing is,

he trips you up!

The good thing is,
he knows just when
to comfort you.

The bad thing is,
he licks your hands,
and then your
face and neck
and ears –

shoo,
puppy!
Shoo!

Sometimes when you call, he will not come.

And then you have to call and call, and look for him.

But when you find
your puppy,

you're so glad!

The best thing is,
a puppy is a friend.

Woof! Woof!
Get off me, pup!

Giggle Club Jokes! No.19
What sound do porcupines make when they kiss?
Ouch!